I want to be just like you.
A Dave The Black Pug book,

Written by Zara Teare
Illustrated by Bex Sutton

With love,
Zara

First Edition 2021

Pug Hugs,

Dave

1

THIS BOOK IS DEDICATED TO YOU!

You are perfect to someone, and that someone should be you.

I WANT TO BE JUST LIKE YOU

Written By
Zara Teare

Illustrated By
Bex Sutton

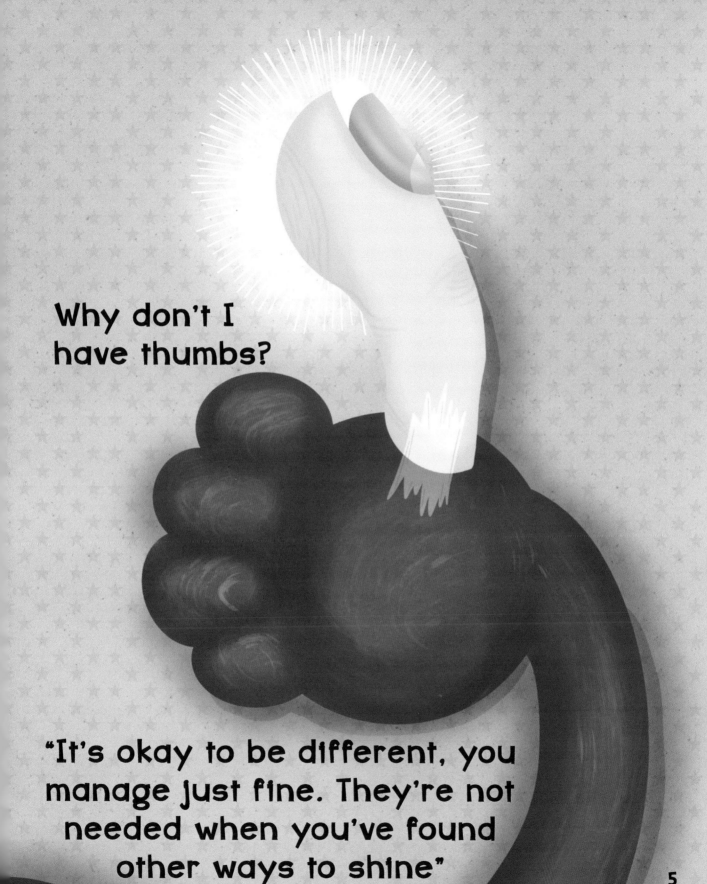

Why don't I
have thumbs?

"It's okay to be different, you
manage just fine. They're not
needed when you've found
other ways to shine"

5

Why am I too short?

"It's not good to all be the same. some people are tall, there is no one to blame."

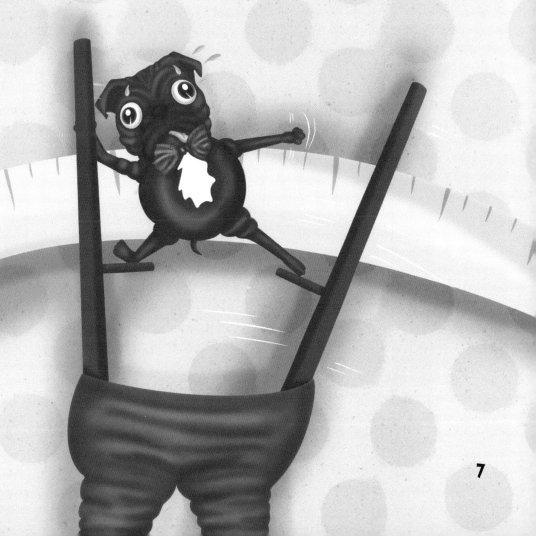

Why am I wrinkly?

"That's how you are, it's a beautiful face. Look in the mirror and learn to embrace."

ANTI WRINKLE CREAM

HOW TO GET RID OF WRINKLES!

HOW DOES SHE LOOK SO YOUNG!

Why am I not clever?

$$E = MC^2$$

"That's not true, we all learn at a different pace. To be intelligent is not a race."

Why don't I like swimming?

"There is no rule to like the same as your friend, you enjoy different things, so start your own trend."

Why do my eyes look funny?

"This makes you unique, your eyes are so pretty. They tell a story, making you charming and witty."

Why does my tail curl?

"Have you ever noticed, it makes us all smile."

"Be confident, it's you, I'm in love with your style."

Why do I sometimes worry?

"We need to show feelings, I know you can be shy. Please remember it's okay if you need a hug and cry."

Why am I turning grey?

"It's a wonderful thing, growing up to be old, remember your journey and all the stories to be told"

Why do they call me ugly?

"A bully will name call,
but please try to ignore.
It's not you, it's them,
when they feel insecure."

23

Why do you say no?

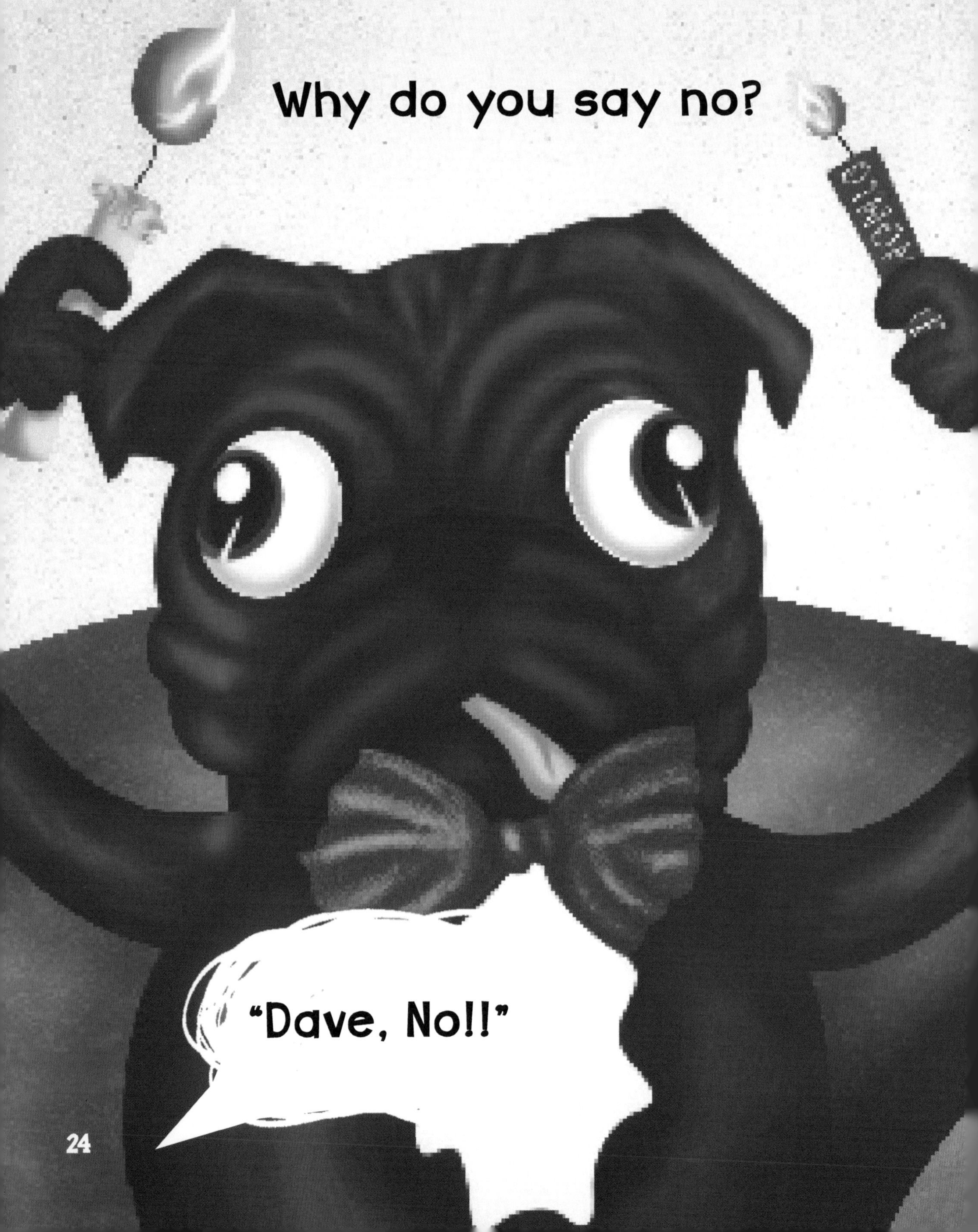

"Your cuteness let's you get away with many things. You can't have everything no matter how much you whinge."

"No Dave!"

I want to be just like you!

"Talk to someone, it will help you
get through. We all have those
days when we feel a little blue.
I am not perfect, there is no such
thing. We face each day and the
adventure life brings.

You might feel different and not like what you see. Please remember I love you, and you are perfect to me"

Did you enjoy Dave the Black Pug's adventure?
Read his first book:

I WANT TO BE A PUGLEBRITY

The first book in a sweet and funny new series about Dave The Black Pug and Mummy, Who are trying to solve one of the hardest questions of his life.

What should he be when he is older?

Dave the black pug is adventurous, ambitious and determined! Although sometimes in life, things aren't always as simple as that.

When I grow up, I want to be a Motor Racer.

With the advice of his human, Dave dreams big, focuses and believes, something we all do when we're young, but when it comes to time to choose, I wonder what Dave will become?

Bursting with stunning illustration throughout, this comical children's book is not to be missed!

Zara Teare & Dave The Black Pug

Zara Teare is a poet, writer and author of a Dave The Black Pug book "I want to be a Puglebrity".

Zara has a National Diploma in Performing Arts- Plymouth College, where she found her love for the art industry, script writing and creating characters.

She lives and works out of her home in Eggbuckland, Plymouth. Zara spends her time making memories with her husband, step son and their pug Dave.

Zara enjoys spending time with Dave and eating cake. Dave enjoys spending all his time with his family, his favourite things are chicken, sticking his tongue out and being next to Mummy.

Bex Sutton Illustrator

Bex Sutton is a UK based illustrator who works on a variety of projects. With the company of her husband, two cats and giant puppy, she can be found illustrating day and night on her computer, losing herself in a new magical world she designs.

She can be reached by email at bex@primalst.com

Fun Facts!

Did you know chocolate is toxic to dogs? That's why Mummy tells Dave 'No!' When he's eating chocolate!

Did you know the painting where Dave is a beautiful woman is based on a real painting? It's called 'The Birth Of Venus' and was painted by Sandro Botticelli in 1486.

Fun Facts!

Did you recognise who Dave dressed up as here?

It was Albert Einstein!

Born 1879, he was one of the most famous scientists to exist! During his life he thought of many theories about light, gravity, space and time. He also won a Nobel Prize!

Did you know the smallest living dog in the world is less than 10cm tall!

A Female Chihuahua called Milly is the smallest living dog measuring at 9.65cm. That's smaller than your average ruler! We don't think Dave is very short now!

Fun Facts!

Did you know some dogs are faster than cheetahs?

That's right! Although cheetahs can reach 70mph, they can only run that fast for a short amount of time, where as Greyhound dogs can run at 35mph for 7 miles, meaning they would outrun a cheetah!

Did you know the tallest dog to live was 1.118m on all fours, 2.23m when standing on two paws! That's 7 ft 4 in tall! His name was Zeus and he was a Great Dane.

What is the most intelligent dog breed according the scientists?

After testing 200 professional dogs, scientists found the most intelligent of all dog breeds is the Border Collie!

Printed in Great Britain
by Amazon